Lola Plants a Garden

Mary, Mary, quite contrary,
how does your garden grow?
With silver bells
and cockleshells
and pretty maids all in a row.

For Suzanne: every garden should have such a splendid bloom—A. McQ.

To Ethan and Frankie with love—R. B.

First published in the United Kingdom in 2014 by Alanna Books,
46 Chalvey Road East, Slough, Berkshire, SL1 2LR, United Kingdom,
as Lulu Loves Flowers. Copyright © 2014 Alanna Books.

ISBN 978-0-545-85364-4

21 22 23 24 25   40   29 28 27 26 25 24 23 22

Printed in the U.S.A.

First Scholastic printing, February 2015

Illustrations done in acrylic on paper
Display type set in Garamouche Bold
Text type set in Billy by SparkyType
Designed by Martha MacLeod Sikkema

Scholastic Inc., 557 Broadway, New York, NY 10012

Lola Plants
a Garden

Anna McQuinn
Illustrated by Rosalind Beardshaw

SCHOLASTIC INC.

Lola loves her book of garden poems.
Her favorite poem
is the one about Mary Mary.

Lola wants to plant a garden. Mommy says there is room near the vegetables.

3

Lola gets books about
gardens from the library.

She chooses her favorite flowers from the books.

Mommy makes a list.

They go to the
garden store to buy seeds.

Lola and Mommy make the garden.

The seed packets mark
where the flowers are planted.

Lola will have to wait
a long time for them to grow.

9

Lola makes her own flower book
while she waits.

Mommy types the Mary Mary poem, and Lola glues it in.

11

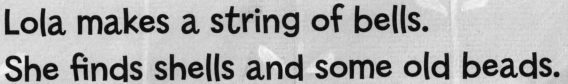

Lola makes a string of bells.
She finds shells and some old beads.

12

She even makes
a little Mary Mary.

13

One day Lola sees tiny green shoots!

14

She pulls up weeds
so the shoots can grow.

Lola's flowers grow bigger.
They open up to the sun.

16

Daddy helps Lola hang her shiny bells.

18

Lola finds Mary Mary a special spot.
It's just perfect.

Orla, Ben, and Ty are coming
to see Lola's garden.
Lola and Mommy make cupcakes.

Lola wears her flower shirt.
Mommy helps Lola with her hair.

21

Lola's friends love everything about her garden.

They share the crunchy peas
and sweet strawberries
that Mommy grew.

Then Lola makes up a story about Mary Mary.

24

What kind of garden will
Lola plant next?

25

Lola, Lola, extraordinary,
how does your garden grow?
With flower seeds
and shells and beads
and happy friends all in a row.